In this wonderful short story, you'll take a journey through more than two dozen life-changing biblical principles that illustrate why the only way to ride is with Jesus as your guide!"

—Josh D. McDowell, Author/Speaker

A great new look at a very old concept, told by a guy whose surrendered life is a testimony to God's grace.

—Sandy Rios, President of Concerned Women for America

This powerful little parable is all about the sheer, exhilarating joy of taking your hands off the handlebars and lifting your feet high off the pedals—to enjoy the ride of your life!

—Wayne Shepherd, Host of *Open Line*, Moody Broadcasting

This is the kind of story that will haunt you for the rest of your life, until you climb into the backseat of your own "bike built for two" and see a whole new world. This little book is dynamite and just might change your life.

—Steve Brown, Author, Professor and Bible Teacher on *Key Life*

Jay has so simply and powerfully captured the journey of life! So many of us are slow to learn the simple lesson of this fable. May this short story help many to move quickly to the passenger's seat.

—Dann Spader, Executive Director of SonLife Ministries

I love to hear old stories told in fresh ways. Jay has done just that in this life-changing story! Read it. It could change your life!

—Dan Seaborn, Executive Director of Winning at Home Ministries

Once Upon
A Tandem

a modern fable retold by
Jay K. Payleitner

illustrations by
Rex Bohn

HOWARD
PUBLISHING CO.

Our purpose at Howard Publishing is to:

* *Increase faith* in the hearts of growing Christians
* *Inspire holiness* in the lives of believers
* *Instill hope* in the hearts of struggling people everywhere

Because He's coming again!

Once Upon A Tandem © 2003 by Jay K. Payleitner
All rights reserved. Printed in the United States of America

Published by Howard Publishing Co., Inc.
3117 North 7th Street, West Monroe, Louisiana 71291-2227

03 04 05 06 07 08 09 10 11 12   10 9 8 7 6 5 4 3 2 1

Edited by Philis Boultinghouse
Cover and interior design by LinDee Loveland
Illustrations by Rex Bohn

ISBN: 1-58229-337-6

Dedicated to
Rita, *my love*

The author wishes to acknowledge and thank all those who directly or indirectly have made an impact on this little book, including: Alec, Randy, Max, Isaac, Rae Anne, Marge, Ken, Mary Kay, Mark, Sue, Chrys, John, Denny, Philis, LinDee, Rex, Joe, Paul, Angela, Paul, Charles, Hildred, Jim, Dan, Bernie, Frank, Steve, Dan, Tim, Jim, Ed, Tim, Jann, Julie, Tim, Sandy, Chuck, Dan, John, Rudy, Dave, Josh, Steve, Philip, Jesus, all those who originated and perpetuated this story, and any reader who shares this book with a friend. The Web site onceuponatandem.com details these contributions.

He is no fool
who gives what he cannot keep
to gain what he cannot lose.
—Jim Elliot

PREFACE

Several years ago, someone—I forget who—shared with me a simple story that cast new light and new insight on my life journey.

The story came to me at just the right moment, at a time when I was jumping through too many hoops and asking more than my share of questions. That simple story—nothing more than a word picture really—brought sweet clarity to my life. To be sure, I didn't understand all the theological implications involved, but I did finally know what I had to do.

And now, I offer this story to you. With this writing, I've added a few twists and turns to the original word-of-mouth tale. But I trust the purity and integrity of the original shines through.

Did you ever see
a bicycle built for two...

with only one rider?

It looks kind of like there's
an invisible person riding
on the back.
The back pedals go around,

but there's nobody there.

It reminds me of the way
my life used to be.
It was like I had a nice
big bike for two,
but I certainly wasn't ready

to share it.

Every place I went,
I rode all by myself.
No one could tell
me what to do
or where to go.

And I liked it like that.

But then something
stirred inside me.
Or rather, something
echoed through my
hollow heart.

I came to realize
that the empty seat
shouldn't stay empty.
After all, tandem bikes
are built for two.

Indeed, as the miles
dragged by, it
became increasingly
evident that I was
spinning my wheels
for no reason at all,
and maybe,

just maybe...

that empty back seat
had something to do
with my empty heart.

So I began to consider
the idea of picking up
one of the many hitch-
hikers along the way.

Some were well dressed.

Most were not.

Some called out in
lyrical voices—

even calling me by name.

Many of them,
simply by their
disturbing
appearance,
provoked me
to speed up

and *race by.*

For a few,
I s l o w e d a l m o s t to a halt.

Collectively, they were
short, tall, smiling, scowling,
alluring, and aloof. In their
hands or on their backs were
threadbare bags, suspicious-
looking bundles,
sleek briefcases,
and gigantic trunks.

Some traveled with
nothing at all.

One hitchhiker
looked like a best
friend I hadn't seen
in years.

Another wasn't trying
to hitch a ride at all,
but his hand-lettered
sign told me he was
quite eager to trade his
single-seat racing bike
for my twin-seated
tandem.

I passed them all.

I did not stop.

And it began to
look like my
expedition would
be solo

after all.

But then one day,
on the crest of a
slight hill,

I did stop.

For him.

Please don't ask why.

Looking back, I
surprised even
myself when I
invited him to
share my bike
and my journey.

But something told me
(maybe even he told
me, I forget) that he
would be the perfect
companion.
So I invited him on.

And we rode.

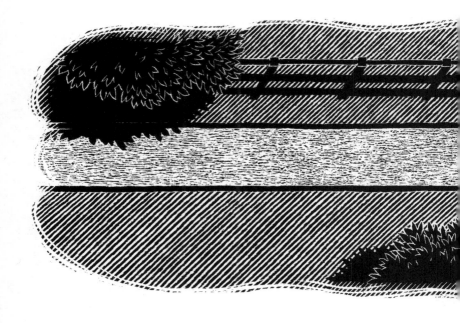

He and I.

But what's this?

Perhaps, I'd made a mistake

—a huge one.

My new bikemate isn't pedaling.

He's **deadweight.**

I'm working harder than ever, and

he's slowing me down.

Not surprisingly, I begin
to wonder why I ever let
him on in the first place.
Finally, I turn and say,

"How come you never pedal?"

With a wink
and a smile,

he replies,...

"I thought you'd never ask."

And so life is better.

Easier.

Pedaling with my new
colleague, the miles
breeze by. I reach my
daily traveling objectives
more quickly than ever.

Still, there's something incomplete about this arrangement. When we arrive at my carefully chosen destinations, they are never as satisfying as I imagined they'd be. As soon as we arrive, I find myself wishing I were

someplace else.

No amount of map
reading, atlas studying,
or advance planning is
ever enough.
I remain unsettled,
always hoping that
better things are waiting just over the next hill.

Then on an
overcast day—better
suited to sitting by a
fire than riding a bike
—suddenly

the sun breaks through.

At this moment, I
realize that my traveling
companion has been
whispering directions to
me the whole time.
I hadn't heard him
because I was too busy
with my own plans.

Now, when I take his
advice, we wind up
on short cuts
and smooth roads,
and all roads
seem to go d o w n h i l l .

Even when his
directions contradict
everything I'd learned
before we met, his very
presence gives me the
courage to forge ahead.

Despite my doubts
and fears, I find
myself bicycling
down strange roads
that are not even on
my maps.

I am learning to listen.

To trust.

To have faith.

Then, when I get
tired of pedaling, I
put my feet up on the
handlebars. And as it
turns out—

I've been slowing him down!

He never gets tired
and all I have to do,
it seems, is keep
my ears tuned to
his directions.

Nothing, I decide, could
be better than tandem
biking like this. That
back seat—the one that I
so hesitated to fill—
was clearly meant for this

counselor,
          brother,
                    and friend.

But, once again,
I'm wrong.
Believe it or not—
I discover something
even better.

It becomes clear that
he shouldn't be riding
along and whispering
in my ear from the
back seat.

That's not where he belongs.

You see, the real
adventure begins when I
stop the bike and invite
him to take my place
—the front seat—

handlebars and all.

In the twinkling of
an eye, I realize
that he not only
knows the road,

he owns it.

Every breathtaking
view and every
eye-opening
discovery,

he chooses especially for me.

And my oh my, the places he takes me.

The sights I see.

The scenic routes.

The unexpected detours.

The dizzying mountaintops.

The green valleys.

All places I would have missed.

Furthermore, this new
perspective—looking just
over the shoulder of my
traveling companion—gives
me a bold, new confidence.

I trust his vision knowing
that he sees not only the
next hill, but all the hills
and curves

　　　　　that lie ahead.

What's even more amazing
is that sometimes we end
up on strange, perilous
roads strewn with rocks
and brambles. Or we are
momentarily mired in mud
and quicksand.

When I least expect it, he may even maneuver our tandem bicycle through a dark, narrow tunnel.

But through it all, his
calm becomes my calm.
His strength becomes
my strength.

I know without a
twinge of doubt that he
would never allow
even the bumpiest road
to jar me from my seat.

And, yes, on occasion, he asks me to pedal. I know he doesn't really need my help, but gritting my teeth and pumping my legs for all I'm worth is just what I need to stay strong and

focused for the journey.

Oh, I still have my
own handlebars and,
to be sure, sometimes

I hang on for dear life.

But on a tandem
bike, those back
handlebars

can't steer at all.

So I go where he goes.

And I wouldn't have it any other way.

*"Whoever finds his life
will lose it, and whoever
loses his life for my sake
will find it."*

Matthew 10:39

For a fresh perspective on your own
life journey or for a glimpse of
what's just over the next hill,
visit the Web site:
onceuponatandem.com